IT RAINED WARM BREAD

IT RAINED WARM BREAD

Moishe
Moskowitz's
Story of Hope

story by
GLORIA MOSKOWITZ-SWEET
poems by
HOPE ANITA SMITH
with illustrations by LEA LYON

Christy Ottaviano Books
Henry Holt and Company • NEW YORK

*I swore never to be silent whenever and wherever
human beings endure suffering and humiliation.
We must take sides.*

—ELIE WIESEL

*It is not our differences that divide us. It is our inability
to recognize, accept, and celebrate those differences.*

—AUDRE LORDE

Henry Holt and Company, *Publishers since 1866*
Henry Holt® is a registered trademark of Macmillan Publishing Group, LLC
120 Broadway, New York, NY 10271 • mackids.com
Text copyright © 2019 by Gloria Moskowitz-Sweet and Hope Anita Smith
Illustrations copyright © 2019 by Lea Lyon
All rights reserved.

Library of Congress Cataloging-in-Publication Data
Names: Moskowitz-Sweet, Gloria, author. | Smith, Hope Anita, author. | Lyon, Lea, 1945– illustrator.
Title: It rained warm bread / story by Gloria Moskowitz-Sweet ; illustrations by Lea Lyon.
Description: First edition. | New York : Henry Holt and Company, 2019. | "Christy Ottaviano Books." |
Summary: A fictionalized account of the experiences of a Polish Jew, Moishe, who with his parents, brother, and sister, struggles to survive the Nazi invasion and Holocaust.
Identifiers: LCCN 2018039243 | ISBN 9781250165725 (hardcover)
Subjects: LCSH: Holocaust, Jewish (1939–1945)—Poland—Juvenile fiction. | Jews—Poland—Juvenile fiction. | World War, 1939–1945—Poland—Juvenile fiction. | CYAC: Novels in verse. | Holocaust, Jewish (1939–1945)—Poland—Fiction. | Jews—Poland—Fiction. | World War, 1939–1945—Poland—Fiction. | Poland—History—Occupation, 1939–1945—Fiction.
Classification: LCC PZ7.5.M67 It 2019 | DDC [Fic]—dc23
LC record available at https://lccn.loc.gov/2018039243

Our books may be purchased in bulk for promotional, educational, or business use. Please contact your local bookseller or the Macmillan Corporate and Premium Sales Department at (800) 221-7945 ext. 5442 or by email at MacmillanSpecialMarkets@macmillan.com.

First edition, 2019 / Designed by Rebecca Syracuse
Printed in the United States of America by LSC Communications, Harrisonburg, Virginia

1 2 3 4 5 6 7 8 9 10

For my father, Michael Moskowitz, and to all those who refuse to turn a blind eye to injustice.

—Gloria Moskowitz-Sweet

This book is dedicated to Michael (Moishe) Moskowitz. Thank you for trusting me with your story. It is powerful, painful, and beautiful.

—Hope Anita Smith

For Bernie, who shared my journey through this important project with love and support.

—Lea Lyon

Contents

CHAPTER 1

IT MATTERS

1936

IT MATTERS

It matters
which side of the street
I walk on to get home.
There is their side,
and the safe side,
the only side that gets me home
the same way my mother sent me out.

It matters
that my eyes are watching,
scanning the neighborhood for
thirsty Polish boys,
who drink Jews like water,
wanting
to pound me like schnitzel.

It matters
that I have learned the politics
of life.

Know enough to find two Goliaths

to protect me.

My contribution:

homework assignments worthy of a good grade.

My teacher gives us an exercise.

"Write something that has meaning.

Use your shovel.

Dig deep."

I want to say something important.

Something that will last.

Something that says I was here.

I write my name.

Moishe Moskowitz.

I matter.

SMALL WORLD

Our world is small.
Our life is simple.
We live in the house
my father got as a wedding gift
from my mother's parents.
There are two rooms
and five of us.
My brother and I sleep with our father
and my sister shares a bed with our mother.

I go to two schools,
public school and Hebrew school.
I walk one hour each way,
my legs are able.
I speak two languages,
Polish and Yiddish.

My mother stays home
washing, cleaning, cooking.

I bring in water
and chop wood to heat our house.

I am a good son.

My sister, Bella,
is like her name.
She is beautiful.
She has our mother's face.
My brother, Saul,
is too old for games.
He sits with the men
rocking and chanting prayers.

My father travels.
He is gone most of the week.
It takes many days to buy a cow.
He makes sure to be home for the Sabbath.

My mother and Bella light the candles.
Together we say prayers,
thanking the Master of the Universe
for our small world
and our simple life.

NOT SO BAD

We live in Poland,
a country that has no use for us.
A country that bullies its citizens,
beats up on us because we are different.
Living in Kielce, we are familiar
with being unfamiliar.
I had a hatred for Poles and all things Polish.
They destroyed our property,
burned our homes,
and every Friday
Catholic boys lie in wait to smear pork fat
on our faces as we walk home to
prepare for Shabbat.

My father wipes my face and says,
"It's not the best thing, Moishe,
but if this is the worst thing, it's not so bad."

IN PREPARATION

Mother scents the house
with blueberry pierogi
warm from the oven.
The Sabbath is coming.
We are in preparation.
Outside, I chop wood for the stove.
Bella helps in the kitchen,
and Saul,
too tired to remove the threads
clinging to him from the tailor's shop,
is home just in time for dinner.
We are all present and accounted for.
A blessing.
I see us wrapped in the glow of the Shabbos candles.
We are light.
My mother says the prayer.
My sister mouths the words.
She is in preparation, too.
Later, we walk to temple

and I am still warm
from the meal my mother made,
the words my father spoke,
and the light from the candle's flame.

LESSONS LEARNED

I study hard.
I want to be
an educated man,
like my father.
I'm a fast learner.
I write out my lessons neatly
and quickly,
then tuck them in my schoolbag,
excited to share what I've learned.
But every day is the same.
My teacher, Mr. Bienkowski,
asks a question
and my hand shoots up
like a rocket,
but Mr. Bienkowski can't see me

(even with his glasses on).

He calls on someone else.

Someone who doesn't raise his hand.

Someone who doesn't know the answer.

He has taught me that I am wasting my time,

but I keep trying.

I want Mr. Bienkowski to know

I'm ready, whenever he decides to call on me.

But he never does.

Each time he passes over me

it's like an invisible punch in the stomach

and it hurts more than anything

the Polish boys could do to me.

I'm sure he didn't mean to,

but Mr. Bienkowski has taught me something else:

Bullies come in many shapes and sizes.

A SWEET TREAT

After school my mother makes me a
sugar sandwich
using bread that she and Bella have baked.
My mother knows that I need something
to curb the bitter taste of
Polish boys in my class
who hate
not me
but the thing that makes me different—
I am a Jew.
In Hebrew school I am taught
that we are The Chosen People
and I feel it.
I am sandwiched between two Polish boys
who keep me safe for a price.

No boy has ever struck me.

They hate me only with their eyes.

It leaves a bad taste in my mouth.

My sandwich is toasted, warm,

with just enough sugar to sweeten my day.

IN THE MIDDLE

In my family, I am in the middle.

Stuck between two tall towers that are my

younger sister and my older brother.

My sister is still too young for chores and cooking.

She is content to play and giggle with her friends.

She is concerned with nothing.

My brother's forehead is creased with worry like our father's.

He has forgotten how to laugh.

"You don't know how to have fun anymore," I tell him.

"You are too busy trying to be a man."

"I am a man," he replies, chest out.

My father watches me.

He knows.

He knows that I know.

Everything is changing.

CHAPTER 2

THEY'RE COMING

1939

THEY'RE COMING

The color of the sky is changing.

I lie awake at night

listening to my parents' voices.

Their words tiptoe across the air.

"They are coming," my father whispers.

My mother says to him,

"You must go to America, like your brother.

Then send for us."

Her words are urgent.

They rush about.

I feel a cool wind blow into the room.

My father's reply is a sharp axe.

"I will not leave you," he says.

"I will not leave our children.

The wolves are coming."

I pull the covers over my head.

The Nazis are not here yet,

but fear has already captured us.

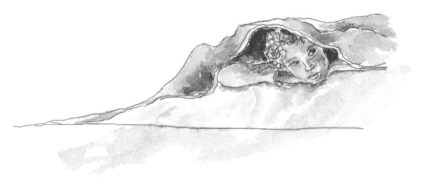

JANEK

My father's friend Janek
has a farm.
When I was younger,
Father would take me with him to visit.
While the men talked business over hot tea,
I played with Janek's dog.
Today when he prepares to go to Janek's house
I am not invited to come along.
I already know that this visit is
between friends.
My father stands in the dirt outside of our house.
He looks as if he has brought his troubles to ask his wiser self
what we should do.
Mother comes out with a bag of food.
It is filled with latkes for Janek.

She places it in my father's hands

and their hands hold on to each other

before Father pulls away and starts down the road.

"What is the food for?" I ask my mother.

"It is a thank-you," she says.

"Your father has a difficult favor to ask of Janek."

"What if . . . ," I ask,

pausing to breathe in the last of the scent

of my mother's delicious treat,

"What if he says no to the favor?

Will Father bring the latkes back to us for dinner?"

I am hopeful when I ask this.

My mother turns to me, laboring to push her mouth

up into a smile.

"No, Moishe. The food is for Janek, whether he says yes or no.

It is not a thank-you for the favor,

it is a thank-you for his friendship."

LETTING GO

My mother is nervous.
She wrings her hands,
wet towels that need to be dried.
Her mouth is turned down at the corners
as if it is too weary to raise itself up into a smile.
Every day she packs away one of her favorite things.
She tells Bella, Saul, and me that we must do the same.
Bella doesn't understand and hides her books and toys
under the bed.
My mother finds them and puts them in the box.
Bella cries, but our mother is resolute.
"Every day," she says as she gently but firmly
moves Bella out of her way,
"we must stop loving something.
If the worst should happen,
we will need to hold on to what is most important:
the love we have for each other."

HIDING

Today we are all headed to
Janek's house.
My father leading the way,
Bella riding on Saul's shoulders,
and my mother and me behind them.
We don't talk,
only force our mouths to become
commas lying on their backs
looking up at the sky
to anyone we meet along the way.
We hope our faces say,
this is a day
just like any other day.

Janek comes out to meet us.
My father jumps over the greeting and
gets right to the point.
"We must hide."
Janek nods.

Herds us off behind his house
to the barn.
It is dark and the dust swarms
like a hive of bees
at even the slightest movement.
The hay is a million needles
pricking us at every opportunity.
From our hiding place, I can hear
Janek's dog barking, calling me to play.
I am feeling guilty.
I wish I had been more friendly—
Janek will keep our secret,
but his dog has no such loyalty to us.
The barn smells.
"What did you think?" Saul asks.
"It's a barn," Bella says,
and buries her nose in our mother's dress.
"You'll get used to it," Father says.
We settle in.

No playing.
No light at night.
No conversations.

I no longer go to school,

and still,

I have mastered a new subject.

I have learned to be invisible.

LESSONS LEARNED

Two months hiding in a barn.

Without speaking.

And yet, we have learned sixty new words for fear.

Monday—worry

Tuesday—panic

Wednesday—dread

Sixty words for sixty days.

After dark, we are bold.

Leave fear in the barn,

forget the worries of our lives.

Go out into the night and

dare to look the stars in the eye.

Someone might see us.

Someone might tell.

Our eyes dart right and left.

We see shadows moving all around us.

Each time,

we forget to breathe.

We are so hungry for home

we cannot think clearly.

GOING TO THE MOVIES

"A barn is not a home."
These are the words of my sister, Bella.
The barn is dark, smells of cows,
and the hay is itchy.
Bella is miserable and too little
to hide it.
Her complaining stops only long enough
for her to cry.
When I see the tears in her eyes about to
spill over,
I grab her hand.
"Shhh. Come with me, Bella."
I help her up the ladder to the loft
and lay my coat down
as a blanket over the hay.

"What are we doing?" she whimpers.

"I wanted to take you to the movies.
Lie down."

I lie down beside her and search until
I find what I'm looking for.

"There," I say, pointing up at a spider
hard at work on a web.

"What's it called?" she asks as she
leans her head against my shoulder.

"This one," I say, "is called
The Adventure of the Web Weaver."

TOO SOON

A visitor comes to see Janek.
Another farmer.
A friend.
"I have news," he says.
I am listening to everything he says.
He tells Janek and my father that
the Nazis have come,
but they aren't bothering anyone.
All is quiet on the outskirts of Kielce.
My father blushes
at his extreme measures.
Two months hiding in a barn.
My mother touches his arm.
We say good-bye to Janek.
Thank the barn occupants

for sharing their home.

They roll their eyes,

chew clumps of hay.

Good riddance, they say as they

spread out into the space we've left behind.

We are delirious.

We are going home.

We were not thinking clearly.

We went home too soon.

UNINVITED GUESTS

Our uniformed visitors
were like guests who didn't know
the party was over.
They stayed.
The city of Kielce housed the largest population
of Jews in Poland.
And yet, the wolves loomed large, overshadowed us.
Not more,
but mighty.
There was something
about them,
something that said they weren't visitors,
something not quite human.
Their eyes followed us,
as if we were something good to eat.
We forgot who we were.
Skittered around like rabbits
trying to make ourselves small.
If we saw one Nazi soldier,

we knew there were others close by.

They loped about,

their noses pointed toward the sky

as if they were trying to pick up a scent.

We admired our shoes, the ground beneath our feet.

We dared not look into their eyes.

We looked down

in submission

and backed away slowly.

With each fearful step we thought we were giving them

Kielce.

But we were wrong.

They were taking it.

BULLIES TO BEASTS

The wolves had been quietly marking our territory

for their own

with the urine of our blood and

the scat of our bodies.

Letting us know

this place was theirs.

I had learned from my father's many books

that the world was big.

How much could wolves need?

Want?

Demand?

They moved with a confidence

as sharp as their teeth,

covering many square miles.

We didn't know yet

(and some would never know)

that we were not the only ones.

Others

from nearby towns

had met with the same fate.

We forgave ourselves

for not knowing.

We'd never thought to study wolves.

Had no idea how horrible they could be.

They were bullies transformed into beasts.

Yes,

there were rumors,

but even my father,

so like Solomon,

could not have imagined such evil.

MAIL

Letters arrived.
Small, white envelopes that held the voices
of our family in Chicago.
Grandfather Israel, Uncle Abraham, and Uncle Jacob.
COME TO AMERICA.
It wasn't an invitation,
it was a plea.
A chance.
America was watching,
could see by their blank hollowed-out
faces that something in the wolves
had been starved.
Now they were ravenous,
would stop at nothing to fill

that empty place.

Inside one envelope,

a ticket and papers

wrapped inside a letter like a present.

COME. TO. AMERICA.

But my father wouldn't leave us.

My father tossed each chance aside.

He did not want to believe

what our American family already knew.

COME.

Urgency inked into the thin white paper.

Grandfather Israel, Uncle Abraham, and Uncle Jacob

kept writing,

their voices quiet but insistent.

The news had traveled all the way to Chicago.

And they were sending it back to us.

"Don't you know?

The wolves are on the attack."

COME.

All of us at once?

Neyn. Es iz faran nisht genug gelt.

No. There is not enough money.

There is a job waiting for you.

You'll find a place to stay.
In no time at all,
you'll have enough to send for
Golda, Bella, Moishe, and Saul.
Trust us.
Wolves will not bother with
women and children.
They will be fine.
But you have to
COME.
NOW.

My father could stand it no longer.
Every day scribbles on pieces of paper
were pushing him toward America.
His suitcase was already packed.
There was no time for long goodbyes.
He kissed each of us,
held my mother close,
and whispered something in her ear.
Tears were streaming down her face,
but she smiled.
And then he was gone.
But before we had a chance to miss him,

he was back.

The borders were closed.

There was no way out.

My father had waited too long

to take his last chance.

COUNSELOR

Whenever there was a problem . . .
What to plant?
How to make a cow well?
How to get an ornery goat to give milk?
Who to marry a son or daughter off to?
My father had the answer.
He was a learned man.
Wise, like Solomon.
People would arrive
outside our house
carrying their troubles in their hands,
or their fear.
My father would listen,
and the answers that didn't come easy
made him pace back and forth
until he wore a path in the dirt.
He would walk and it was as if his steps
unearthed the answer.
I would watch from the window
as each person left

lighter than when they arrived.

Their burdens lifted.

But now that the wolves are here

my father's footsteps

bring no answers to light.

Only dirt rises from the ground under his feet.

And when the dust clears,

the wolves surround us.

CHAPTER 3

WOLVES AT THE DOOR

WOLVES AT THE DOOR

The Nazi soldiers have built a den in our town.

They are wolves traveling in packs.

They are hungry.

Neighbors are disappearing.

There are beatings and

public humiliations.

They are eating Jews.

We become shadows.

Try not to draw attention to ourselves.

Be still.

Don't breathe.

All we can do is watch,

recording every offense.

Soldiers, foaming at the mouth

as they destroy businesses and houses

and people.

Our Polish neighbors watch, too,

but only for a moment.

They must make a choice:

Bury their heads in the sand

or pick up a fistful and throw it at us.

The Nazis devise a plan

to make it easier to find their prey.

By candlelight,

my mother sews yellow patches

on our jackets and coats.

We are stars,

but we do not shine.

NOT ENOUGH STARS

The wolves are howling.

They come out at night

sniffing within the walls of the ghetto.

"One of you, come with us."

In every house,

someone is taken.

A father.

A son.

A brother.

There are not enough stars in the night sky,

so they snatch those of us

who wear them on our coats.

CORNERED

My brother, Saul, is gone.
Disappeared in the night.
Our mother is frantic.
A limb has been ripped from her.
"My baby! Did they take him?
Is he in prison?"
She has already answered yes
to both of these questions.
My father corners her.
Moves toward her slowly
with soothing sounds.
"Saul is fine," my father says.
"He wanted to do something.
He is strong.
He knew the wolves were hungry for
young men who looked like him.
He left to find help.
This was his chance
to do something.

He took it with my blessing.

I know I'm his father but

I couldn't stop him.

He's seventeen.

He's a man.

He didn't want you to know, Golda, because

he knew you wouldn't let him go.

Hopefully he will make it to Russia.

Be alive."

My mother's relief in Father's words outweighs

her anger.

But now

she keeps me tethered.

Forewarned is forearmed.

ONE FROM EVERY FAMILY

There is much work to be done.
The Nazi soldiers need
more workers.
My brother, Saul, is strong,
but he is not here.
He is a shooting star on a mission.
I stand tall. Chest out.
I am a boy wanting to be a man.
They take my father instead.
Mother and I visit him
every week.
He is working in a big field moving rocks.
I know they are heavy because I can
see the strain in the men's faces and in
their arms as they lift and lug

the rocks to a designated area.

We bring my father food,

but mostly we just bring him us.

The food, he hardly touches,

his stomach punishes him.

He has always had stomach problems.

But he can't get enough of us.

He swallows us up with his eyes.

We know that he is full

each time we leave him.

TRADING PLACES

The next time we see my father,

he is still sick,

has been sick the entire time.

I hardly recognize him and try not

to look frightened.

He can barely stand and his skin hangs

on his body as if it is trying to go somewhere without him.

My mother tells the man in charge

that he must let my father come home

so that she can make him well.

He looks at this David standing in front

of him with a slingshot full of words, and

laughs.

The rule is that each household must offer up a male

to come work.

If she does not have another one,

my father must stay.

My mother closes her mouth.

Her weapon of words cannot slay this Goliath.

I stand tall. Chest out.

I am a boy wanting to be a man.

I dig deep and say,

"I will take his place."

My mother begins to shape her mouth

into a no,

but Father is sick.

I am the only one left.

I am the only man in our house.

Saul is still gone.

Our hope is that he is safely in Russia by now.

She hugs me tightly

and makes the trade.

Me for my father.

MY MOTHER'S BOY

When my mother comes to visit,
she can see that I cannot stay here.
Through my tears, I tell her
everything.
The wolves circle.
They are always nipping at us.
Sometimes they bite.
And sometimes they rip us apart.
The work is hard.
I am grateful for the men who
take up my slack
when the wolves are not watching.
I am hungry for my family.
I want to go home.
My clever mother
has a plan.
She sneaks me out
under her coat.
Wrapped in her arms,

my feet walking in sync with her own,

I breathe in her smell.

We are almost one person.

I can feel her heart pounding

in her chest.

And I can hear her muffled prayer.

She does not ask if she should do this,

she tells the Master of the Universe,

respectfully,

that she is taking me.

We walk right out of the camp.

God has graciously granted her request.

My mother is not a thief.

She has reclaimed me.

I am my mother's boy

a little while longer.

LOCKED ARMS

I wake to the sound
of my mother crying.
In the kitchen,
she's holding my brother in her arms.
Saul is home.
We sit around the table.
Saul tells us his story.
He made it as far as the Russian border.
There was no way out.
Poland's neighbors
have locked arms,
with their backs to us, and will not
let us pass.

BEFORE AND AFTER

BEFORE

We were content.

We always had enough to eat.

"If you have enough to eat, you are wealthy,"

my father said,

and why wouldn't we be?

My father was in the cattle business.

AFTER

I learned that my father was just a man.

Not even a farmer.

He only ever had one cow at a time.

He would go to the country, buy a cow, fatten it up,

and sell it to the butcher.

BEFORE

I knew how to play.
A ball dancing between my feet as
I dashed and darted across our asphalt field
from one goal to another
playing soccer with my friends.

AFTER

The streets were deserted.
There was no dancing.
Father said the music of our youth
had stopped playing.

BEFORE

I thought the men who showed up in our town
were just uniformed tourists
passing through on their way to somewhere
more interesting than our little town.
I smiled into eyes that did not see me.

AFTER ...

PRAYERS

They are trying to erase us
as if we are scribbles on a chalkboard.
They have obliterated our synagogue,
turned it into a warehouse.
I look in the windows,
see pieces of furniture huddled together,
heads bowed as if in prayer.
I wonder if there is a prayer
for protection from wolves.
I know that we are The Chosen People,
but I can't believe we were chosen for this.
Those who pray are arrested
for organizing religious meetings,
their homes demolished.
In our house, led by my father,

my family found a way to talk to God.

We huddled together, heads bowed.

Our prayers were whispered,

sometimes riding on the air we breathe.

We did not know everything, yet we knew this:

The wolves can eat the Jews, but

their mouths are no match for

The Master of the Universe.

CHAPTER 4

THE KIELCE GHETTO

1941

THE GHETTO

It is hard not to be angry at the Maker of the Universe.
We have been ripped from our home
like a Band-Aid from a wound,
so fast, but we are still stinging.
We are herded together into an area,
wooden fencing entwined with barbed wire.
We are marbles on a board.
We roll in whatever direction the wolves tilt us.
We are too many to a room and all of us strangers.
Fear draws us together.
We huddle,
hold on to each other, close our eyes, and pray for sleep,
because there is food,
but only in our dreams.

There is home,

but only in our dreams.

There is school and friends and freedom,

but only in our dreams.

We are caged.

We cannot leave.

We are trapped,

while the animals roam freely.

WE STILL REMEMBER HOW TO PLAY

We are not in our own home,

but Mother

still lights the

Sabbath candles,

blesses our one small room.

I say a prayer for the strangers that surround us

and the rats that scurry about.

On a good day,

my sister makes a doll from straw

and still remembers how to play.

And we all

forget our place in the galaxy,

with our yellow stars.

On a good day, our bellies stop singing their sad refrain

and remember what it is to be full.

On a good day, we remember when the only stars

we knew were the ones up in the sky.

HENRY, A FRIEND INDEED

I thought nothing good
could come from being here in
the Kielce Ghetto,
but I was wrong.
I have found a friend.
"My name is Moishe," I tell him.
"My name is Henry," he says back.
We both speak our names as if they matter.
Henry is small like me.
We make a good team.
Every morning
we go wait at the ghetto gate
for the guard to take us to the labor camp.
We dig trenches.
Shovel sand.

Both of us quick.

Both of us strong.

They call us "little guys,"

but we don't mind.

Today the guard rewards

our hard work.

A loaf of bread for each of us.

Henry and I smile.

We make a good team.

Because of us

our families will be less hungry tomorrow.

UNDER THE WALL

We knew they were coming,
the unwelcome guests we had tried
hard to avoid.
Father was too sick to fight them off,
but Mother distracted them
with rubies and diamonds,
even her gold wedding band.
They were content for a time,
but now they are back.
Father is still ill,
and now Mother's treasure box is almost empty.
Hunger has made itself at home.
Moved in and filled our bellies.
Emptied our minds of reason.
We can barely form a complete thought between us.
But Henry rallies.
He finds a hole,
an eye just big enough for a thin needle of a boy
to pass through.

We wait for nightfall,

then spool me into my father's black coat

with big pockets.

"They shoot smugglers," Henry warns,

but I'm not afraid.

Guided by moonlight,

I thread my way through

the forest to Janek's farm.

Something moves in the darkness.

Wolves?

I sew myself into the night

until we are seamless

and hold my breath.

A rabbit flashes by,

doing what I cannot.

Running for its life.

Shining in the moonlight.

MIDNIGHT MARKET

Once again, our family is asking something of Janek.
Will he help us?
Or will he say
"Enough is enough"?

I should not have worried.
Janek still wears his friendship with my father.
He is nervous,
but not for himself. For me.
He asks about my family
as he leads me to the back of his house.
Janek is thinner.
I can tell that Hunger has come to visit him
a time or two.

Janek does not have much food,
but he gives me as many potatoes as I can carry.
A boy would fill only his pockets,
but I am becoming a man.

I stuff the legs of my knickers.

Fill my shirt.

I keep my hands free.

Extend one to Janek to say

thank you

the way a man would.

The way my father would.

I head back through the dark forest,

squeeze through the opening in the ghetto wall.

Ollie Ollie Oxen Free Free Free.

I am safely back in our prison.

Recaptured by my own hand

with enough food to feed my family for a few more days.

MATHEMATICS

In school,

I did not like math,

and now, I must admit,

I like it even less.

In the ghetto,

even though we are all in the same boat,

we are divided.

Father says we cannot help it.

It is what our minds think we must do to survive.

I look at my father with a question in my eyes.

"Yes," he says, "it is a 'scratch your head' mentality."

We are hungry all the time.

Each day Mother opens up a small velvet pouch and

subtracts a small shiny treasure.

Mother is selling her jewelry to buy us food.

We eat, but it does not take away our hunger.

There is so much sickness.

Hunger is greater than dying, and dying is greater than death.

We are a pie chart,

just like the ones we made in school.

But here, our shaded area keeps shrinking because

The Living are less than The Dead.

We are a word problem the Wolves know how to solve.

DEATH

There is sickness

and sadness

and death.

Death is our all-the-time companion.

There is a corner in the room

reserved for him.

His door is always open.

Father and Mother

cover Bella's eyes.

She has already seen too much that is

not good in the world.

Father, Saul, and I try to stare Death down—

we want him to think

we are not afraid.

Deep down we know

if he invites us over

we will not be able to refuse.

Death does not take "no" for an answer.

CHAPTER 5

THE LIQUIDATION

AUGUST 1942

WEIGHING IN

There is a pounding at the door—
BAM! BAM! BAM!
The wolves are howling:
"Everyone out!
You can take twenty kilograms.
No more!
Move!
Now!"
Our eyes are wide with fear.
Bella is crying.
She clings to her doll.
My mother looks around
the room that is not ours.
There is nothing here that belongs to us.
My mother,

always thinking of her family,

takes a loaf of bread and a few potatoes.

And then my father takes

her hand

and my mother takes

Bella's hand

and Bella takes

Saul's hand

and Saul takes

my hand.

The wolves are

pushing and shoving us out the door.

There is no need for a suitcase.

What we want weighs too much.

We take each other.

DON'T LOOK

The soldiers march us out of the ghetto,
past St. Wojciech Square,
to the waiting trains at Okrzeja Street.
"Moishe, don't look at the soldiers," my father says.
I don't look.
No one in my family looks.
We watch the ground.
I feel as if we are sinking into it—
our fear has weighed us down.

TODAY THE SKY HAS NO COLOR

Today the sky has no color.

I think that's because the sun is on our side.

It is protesting what is being done

to the Jews by refusing to shine.

The air is hot, thick, and still.

BANG!

The sound shatters our ears and

our dear friend David lies on the ground.

Too slow.

BANG!

Too old.

BANG!

Rebellious.

BANG!

Sickly.

BANG! BANG! BANG!

This is a new kind of thunder.

People raining on the ground.

We navigate around the fallen.

Pray the soldiers don't notice Father is sick.

In a lightning flash, Mother's hand leaves my shoulder

and she and my sister are dragged away.

I hear her crying for us, her two sons,

"My children! Who will care for you? Who will feed you?"

I could not see her, but I knew her voice.

I didn't know that these would be the last words I ever

heard from my mother.

We are torn asunder

and a new kind of rain

pours from our eyes.

LAYER BY LAYER

The Nazis peel us like onions,

layer by layer.

Mothers

Fathers

Brothers

Sisters

Family

Friends.

Each time someone is ripped away

a sulfuric gas is released until

the aroma of our sadness stings.

We squeeze our eyes shut tightly,

hoping to burn their memory onto our corneas,

but it is too painful.

All we can do is cry.

THE CHOSEN

In school

it meant something to be chosen.

If you could run fast, kick hard, snatch balls from the sky.

It was an indescribable feeling to find favor with your peers.

But we are not in school.

We are huddled together,

like cattle,

waiting.

And then we are divided up,

as if for teams.

Families are separated.

Women here.

Children here.

Young men over there.

The wolves encircle us.

Some carrying guns

while others hold on to dogs champing at the bit.

There is too much chaos, even, for fear.

The wolves yell.

The dogs growl.

This is the first selection.

We did not know what it meant.

We learned fast.

There was no need to grade on the curve—

even a schlemiel could figure it out.

If your feet move too slowly,

your body is disabled,

or you are guilty of having lived through

too many or not enough years,

you did not make the wolves' team.

At school,

being left for last

made us sad.

But then the bell would ring

and back to class we'd go,

optimistic that tomorrow

we might have a different destiny.

The team not chosen

doesn't have time to feel sad about not being

"good enough."

The wolves raise their weapons and

FIRE!

Saul and I watch as people fall like stones to the ground,

their eyes frozen in surprise.

I wish I could let my father know,

I now understand the meaning of irony.

No CHILDREN HERE

The worst thing is
not knowing.
Where is my father?
My mother? My sister?
Where is my best friend Henry?
When I was small
and I would cry,
my mother,
no matter where she was,
would find me and scoop me into her arms.
She always made me feel safe
and loved.
It was the best part of being a child.
Saul and I are led back to the Kielce Ghetto
in the company of other boys and young men.

We move down streets where nothing is familiar
except their names: Stolarska, Jasna.
There is a stench that causes some to gag.
Others bring up bile.
We must move bodies. But they are stiff and gnarled
like tree branches.
I am not afraid.
The people who lived in these bodies are gone.
We have a job to do—
repair the roads, load coal, clean out the
rooms in the ghetto,
and bury the dead.
With each body we toss into makeshift graves
some of our youth is tossed in, too.
We now know things that only men
could know.
Only men should know.

We are young.
We can see the saltwater
paths that our tears have left on our faces.
We are young,
but we are not children.
There are no children here.

HOPE

Nothing can be bad
when you are looking into the face of
a friend.
Janek has come
wearing hope like a tailor-made suit.
He stands on the other side
of the barbed-wire fence.
"Saul, Moishe,
you're getting out of here."
He is happy to be a messenger
bearing good news.
"Your father is coming for you.
He has joined the resistance."
My ears are hearing,
but my mouth can't move.

Janek has done something
no one has been able to do.
He has given voice to hope.
It feels like the wind has been knocked out of me.

Saul lays his hand on my shoulder
to keep me steady.
I can hardly breathe.
All I hear is
TOMORROW.
HERE.
RESCUE.
FREEDOM.
BE READY.
I've had nothing to be ready for
for a long time.
I need to get that part right because
my father is coming.
For us.

A BRIGHT LIGHT

We can't stop shining.
I'm sure the wolves can see.
We try to tamp down the happiness
dancing around the edges of us.
Keep our heads down to hide
the light in our eyes.
But time goes by slowly.
Tomorrow has stopped to pick flowers
or chat with yesterday
and is in no rush to get *here*.
My father's words sing to me.
"Where there is hope,
there is life."
Knowing my father is coming for us,
that we are worth being retrieved.
Rescued.
We make it through the day
undetected.

TOMORROW NEVER CAME

I wait for my father to come and save us,

though patience and I are not good companions.

Saul and I act as if today is a normal day.

And it is, until . . .

Until it won't be.

Is he close?

Is he almost here?

We are ready.

I will bring nothing with me.

I will need both hands to hug my father,

to hold on to him.

Where is he?

We are ready.

The sun is a Ferris wheel

bringing yesterday around for another spin.

Todays go by so quickly.

And yesterdays are always there to help you reminisce

about the today that is gone

or to trick you into thinking about tomorrow.

Yesterday

I knew that my father was coming.

I waited.

Hope and patience keeping me company.

My father did not come.

Janek said,

Your father will come tomorrow.

My father will come tomorrow.

But this is today.

And suddenly I see how the trick works—

Tomorrow

never comes.

CHAPTER 6

FROM CAMP TO CAMP

1942–1945

FROM CAMP TO CAMP

The location changes.
We are moved from camp to camp,
again and again,
but one thing stays the same—
how hard we work.
All.
Day.
Long.
It gets so cold
our tears freeze.
We once were trees, but now we are twigs.
Some of us have shriveled up
and gone back to the earth from where we came.
Those of us who remain
are a poor excuse for kindling.

I HAVE A PLAN,
LITTLE BROTHER

My brother, Saul,

has a scent, and a sound, and a texture, and a taste,

and a shape.

I experience him with all my senses now.

We are together.

We are luckier than most.

We are blessed.

Saul is three years older.

Back home, we barely acknowledged

each other.

We were strangers

tethered together by blood.

But now we have forged an alliance.

See each other for the first time.

Choose each other every day.

We work side by side

making gunpowder.

A fine mist covers us like a second skin.

We cannot wipe it off;
it has taken root.
When the sun shines through
the window,
we can see tiny particles dancing on air like
deadly little diamonds.
They disguise themselves as air
and we breathe them in.
Guns kill from the outside in,
but this gunpowder has found a way to end us
from the inside out.
I tell Saul
I think we are dying.
He says, "That may be true,
but not here.
I have a plan, little brother."

Now

I see our father in my brother, Saul.

He, too, is a thinker.

Walks through his thoughts.

He has learned patience.

"Are we going?" I ask again.

"Wait," Saul says.

He watches the guards.

They are coming and going.

They are everywhere.

Except when they are not.

Each day Saul reveals small cracks in time

with no guards

that we slip through.

"Are we going?" I ask again.

"Wait," Saul says.

At night he lifts the wooden bunk we sleep on,

me in it,

and then I lift it, empty, over and over

until my arms ache.

"We need to be strong," Saul says.

"Are we going?" I ask.

"Wait," he says.

And then,

one night while I am sleeping

Saul shakes me awake.

I sit up quickly and the only words

I can think to say are,

"Are we going?"

"Yes," Saul whispers.

"Now."

Saul leads as we make our way

through an invisible maze.

We press ourselves into

the sides of barracks,

or into the earth.

He keeps me close.

I know he is determined to get out.

We make it to the fence

unseen.

It is a giant hurdle in front of us.

Our wills lace their fingers together to give

us a leg up.

We run at the barricade and are over it in what seems like

a single bound.

We feel our way through the night.

Are we going?

We are going,

going,

gone.

AND THEN THERE WAS ONE

We were not free.
But we were no longer inside the walls
of that prison.
We stayed hidden during the day.
We had practiced how to be invisible.
We knew the woods well and
traveled only at night.
We were like lost dogs.
We did the only thing we knew to do.
We went back home.
Kielce.
If we could work,
we could live.
Saul and I had gotten strong.

Our strength gave us purpose.

I stayed close to my brother,

following him around like a

second shadow.

He didn't seem to mind.

To look up from our work and see

a familiar face was . . .

everything.

Until.

Saul was out on a work detail

when the wolves showed up

and put me and the others that were there

on a train to Auschwitz.

I did not know that I would never

see my brother, Saul, again,

but I could feel him being ripped away from me

with every *chug-chug* of the train.

I didn't cry.

I couldn't cry.

I had lost the last thing I could lose.

ARBEIT MACHT FREI

When we arrive at

Auschwitz

the gates are opened wide

to receive us.

Above us there is a sign that reads:

ARBEIT MACHT FREI.

WORK SETS YOU FREE.

I wonder how that could be true.

All we have done is work,

and still . . .

There is a man

handpicking people.

Twins.

Anyone cross-eyed.

Anyone with a cleft palate.

"That's Mengele,"

I hear someone say.

"They call him the Angel of Death.

He's picking people for experiments."

"You," Mengele says to a boy with a clubfoot.

We watch as he limps off to the right to join a group there.

I stand to the left with my team.

We stare across at each other.

We are silently asking the question,

Do we want to be where you are?

We don't know.

Neither side is sure which side we want to be on.

IT MATTERs—REPRIsE

The wolves have taken everything

from us.

We own nothing.

But then I remember the one thing that is still mine—

my name.

My name is Moishe Moskowitz.

My name is Moishe Moskowitz.

It belongs to me.

And no matter what the wolves do to me,

my name is mine.

I own it.

I make a point of saying my name

to myself every time I think of what I have lost.

But wolves have keen hearing

and they already had a plan in place

to take even my name from me.

They took us to a huge brick building.

Shoved us inside.

We had to undress down to our shoes.

My name is Moishe Moskowitz.

They shave our heads,

our faces,

our entire bodies.

They strip us of our dignity.

My name is Moishe Moskowitz.

We are sent to another station,

where we are branded

with a number.

I clench my teeth

and try to comfort myself

with my new mantra.

My

B-

My name

6

My name is

4

My name is Moishe

7

My name—

They call me

B-647.

But where there is life, there is hope.

My name is Moishe.

And where there is hope. There is life.

My name is Moishe Moskowitz.

IT MATTERS.

THE SOUP PLATE

Each day the wolves serve up

dry bread and black coffee for breakfast.

Lunch and dinner bring

watery soup.

A soup that will never live up to its potential.

A soup with such low self-esteem

it fills itself up with water.

Diluted, it shrinks away from all that it can be.

I carry my soup plate with me

always.

It is a part of me.

An extra limb.

No soup plate.

No soup.

I don't even notice that it is a plate,

not a soup bowl.
A bowl would corral my soup
with no means of escape.
But a plate
is an open field for my watery soup.
If I do not eat it quickly,
my soup will run to the edge of my plate
and leap off like a wild stallion.
It is not good soup,
but I make sure every drop finds its way
to my mouth.
Hope must be fed.

A GOOD MAN

The wolves come for me.

I can hear their low growl

as they bare their sharp teeth.

I know that I will not be coming back.

Every part of me trembles.

My feet forget what they are supposed to do.

I pull back, but the wolves hold firm.

I can smell my future.

I can smell death.

But before I am dragged across the open field

toward the line of those too sick,

too young, or

too old to work,

a voice calls out—

"Let me keep this one boy.

He is my specialist.

I need him."

Fritz gives me extra soup.

I share it with my hungry bunkmates.

Fritz is a convict from the prison,

not a Nazi.

They use him and others convicted of crimes

to supervise in the camps.

They are called kapos.

They are a step up from us.

And because they have nothing to lose,

they can be vicious.

Because the kapos are

making sure we stay on task,

the wolves go quiet,

lock their teeth back up in their mouths.

Fritz does not look at me,

my eyes so full of gratitude

it is overwhelming.

I hope he sees the good in me.

In this horrible place

I have found

one good person.

Only one.

But when the wolves come to take you away,

one good person is all you need.

WEIGHTLESS

Today,

we are moving mountains,

those who can.

Hefting rocks onto our shoulders

while the rest of the men and boys

walk in a stooped-over position,

too weak to lift their cargo

more than a few inches off the ground.

I surprise everyone.

I transfer rock after rock,

never feeling the weight of my burden,

and I know why.

From the moment we were separated

I have carried them with me.

My beautiful mother.

My erudite father.

My rebellious brother, Saul,

and my wide-eyed little sister, Bella.

They are always with me.

I never put them down.

Carry the thought of them in my heart.

I imagine them safe.

Their images seared into the inside of my eyelids,

their voices, wind chimes in my ears.

To be with them again,

that is my hope.

And as my father would say,

"Where there is hope, there is life."

I tote them around with me everywhere,

the weight of their memory

never so heavy that I would set them down.

I never stop thinking of them.

I carry them.

And because I carry them,

I feel each of them, in turn, reaching out their hands

to lighten my load.

I carry them

and that makes my burden

easier to bear.

DREAM TRAIN

We are finished
for today.
We drag ourselves back to the bunks
in our threadbare pants and shirts.
Wearing (if luck is with us)
old shoes too big for your feet.
Or, if we are clever,
our feet are swaddled in the wrappings
from cement bags.
We trudge through.
It is the only way to get us to our cots.
We are every word for tired.
Some walking with their eyes closed,
letting their feet find their own way.
We are given soup

and struggle to get it down.

We are tired.

Swallowing is yet another task we must undertake.

When my head finally hits the mat,

I close my eyes and sleep comes quickly.

It is a train I have waited for all day.

I jump on.

Grab a window seat.

It will be a short trip.

Morning comes quickly.

My view is always the same.

My mother in the kitchen making pierogi

or turning Bella's tears to laughter.

My father sitting at the table,

solutions to problems rolling out of his brain

on a conveyor belt.

My brother in his "I'm a man" costume.

It all goes by so quickly,

and then I hear the conductor shout,

"Everybody off."

It is time to wake up.

Time to repeat yesterday,

and the day before that, and the day before that.

The conductor yells again, "Last stop!"

Everyone begins to stir.

Look at this scene.

My family landscape.

I press my hand to the glass,

try to touch each family member.

It is time to get up.

Time to disembark.

I am always the last one off

the dream train.

CHAPTER 7

WINTER

1945

HIDING THE EVIDENCE

In the night
we hear whispers of the impossible:
"Americans are coming from the West,
Russians from the East."
The wolves walk around trying to look innocent,
feathers hanging out of their mouths.
Those of us who still have life in us
are marched away at gunpoint
to a faraway camp.
We travel only at night.
The Nazis are thieves,
and we Jews are being stolen.
We feel our way
through the darkness,
through countrysides,

through forests,

and we are given nothing but orders.

March by night. Sleep by day.

No food.

No water.

Our journey looks bleak.

No food. No water.

But we want to survive:

We make our own food and drink.

We drink the dew from blades of grass

and then eat the evidence.

WALKING WITH WOLVES

The wolves are nervous.

There is a lot of commotion.

The younger wolves have left us with the old wolves.

They are worn and tired,

but they are still wolves.

Their teeth are strong.

They march us only at night under

the watchful eye of the moon

and hide us during the day like a well-kept secret.

We can tell that they don't want this job,

they are only following the orders of their pack leader.

These wolves look a lot like us.

They try to make their bodies look small

by flattening their ears against their heads

and tucking their tails between their legs.

There is a lot of commotion.

There is whimpering

and barking.

They seem nervous.

Afraid.

But what have wolves to fear?

And then there is bombing.

Getting louder

and louder

and louder.

I can tell there are some

who are hoping this is the end.

They have no more fight in them.

I am only at the beginning of my story.

If I have to,

I will fight to stay alive.

THE FIRST DEATH MARCH

It is the dead of winter, the dead of night, and
the walking dead.
Someone whispers that we are headed for Germany.
But many know that we are being herded to our deaths.
I don't know how some of the men are able to keep going.
But then I catch sight of their eyes and see they are
anxious to get to Death's house.
He is more merciful than the wolves.
Whenever a man falls to the ground,
the wolves yell for him to
get up.
But Death has him pinned down on the ground and
the man cannot move.

The wolves think he is refusing,
but Death's commands outweigh
anything the wolves say or do.
And then the man lets go
of the balloon that is his life
and it floats away from him.
But it's not enough to be dead.
The wolves jab at the fallen with the butts of their rifles
or the toes of their boots.
If the dead man remains still,
the wolves move on.
I am not satisfied with either option.
So I fall.
There are so many things that could go wrong
with my plan.
I am in shock.
I'm sure I'm not breathing.
They stab me with a bayonet.
I feel it, but I don't even bleed.
Weariness and fear paralyze me.
I don't move.
They kick me.
I still don't move.
Convinced.

The wolves move on.

I am left for dead.

I am afraid to move.

I wait. And wait.

And wait some more.

I get up.

Everyone is gone.

I'm alone.

The sun is shining as I sniff for food like a dog.

And I remember something my mother says—

Hope is a thing with feathers—

I see a farmer.

The farmer sees me.

My striped uniform is my identity tag.

The farmer turns me over to the police.

His eyes never meet mine.

He doesn't want the trouble that comes with helping me.

The death march has passed, so I let myself hope

that I'll be let go.

I think I'm safe.

And then I hear the familiar shuffle of despair.

I turn to see Nazi guards marching by with other prisoners.

They put me in the line.

I march.

Will myself to stay on my feet.

Watch as the thing with feathers

flies away.

CATTLE CARS

The trains stand still on the tracks, snorting like bulls.
We are herded in.
Packed tight.
I am pushed up against the side wall.
I can see out between the boards.
My breath escaping like puffs of smoke.
We no longer know if it is dawn or dusk.
Are we asleep or awake?

The train jerks forward, tossing us about.
We are moving.
Steel wheels clacking.
The outside world goes by in a blur.
Like cattle we stand huddled together
so close that we hold each other up.

We hear a mournful whistle,
long and low.
We cannot tell if it comes from one of us
or the train itself.

THROUGH THE BOARDS

The train stops.

Through the mist we see

a town.

Whispers ripple through the car like water.

"We are in Czechoslovakia."

We are hidden from the world.

The wolves have eaten what was not theirs

and they hide their shame inside

boxcars.

Through the boards we can see.

There is sky and grass and that thing we all cling to . . .

There is life.

The wolves stand tall,

hold their guns at the ready.

They hide their shame inside cattle cars.

No one can see us.

We fight for a chance to look out.

We are like hungry kittens, and what we see

is milk.

We squirm and cram together,

our eyes searching blindly,

searching for a bit of light, sky, grass

to latch on to.

IT RAINED WARM BREAD

When it is my turn
I press the side of my face up
against the boards and become a cyclops.
I am trying to see everything.
My wild eye sees one solid thing
among the many things that are rushing by.
It is a woman.
No, a group of women.
Standing.
And my one wild eye knows
that even though we are unseen . . .
These women SEE us.
They stand still.
They stand out.
They stand up.
For all of us.
Even though the wolves bully them
with their hard eyes and their sharp smiles,
these women see us

and they will not be moved.

And then they are

moved,

are moving,

rushing along,

bundled up against the cold.

Even though they can't see us,

they know.

THEY KNOW.

And these women

in this town

do not turn away.

They turn toward a bakery.

One runs inside.

Others follow.

They come out with arms full.

Something flies into the cattle car.

It is a storm.

At first we are afraid,

Unsure of what is going on.

Our hands reach up

grabbing, pulling.

There is a sweet scent.

And then we know.

It is life.

It is bread,

still warm from the oven.

It is raining warm bread.

We have no table manners.

This is the first time we have eaten in a week.

We devour every loaf,

try to make them disappear before wolves

step in and take them away.

But we don't have to worry.

The wolves do nothing.

THE SCENT OF COURAGE

The train is moving
faster now.
The women from Czechoslovakia are stained into our memory.
Their smell hanging in the air.
It is the scent of courage.
They fed our bodies,
but their willingness to risk
fed our souls.
They did not see wolves that could do them harm.
They saw what the wolves thought they had concealed.
There was something about their eyes that reminded
me of my mother.
I saw love.
Not because we were their sons or husbands or fathers
but just because we were.
We mattered.

REMEMBERING

The bread is gone.
Even its scent
has left the boxcar.
I hold my last piece in my mouth.
I try to make it last forever
or at least until my memory can make the journey
to our lives before the wolves.
My mother is baking bread,
and Bella, who is supposed to be helping,
twirls in her apron like she is a princess.
My brother, Saul, is just a boy,
not a boy wanting to be a man.
He tells me a joke and then
plays checkers with me and lets me win.
I am home.

We have nothing and it is everything,

I can hear my father saying

prayers and it is like music.

Like the bread in my mouth,

the memory is sweet.

It tastes so good and before I can stop myself,

I swallow.

The bread and the memory sink to my stomach

like an anchor.

TRY, TRY, AGAIN
(SECOND DEATH MARCH)

They take us off the trains and
start marching us.
There is a natural selection
as the dead fall away.
We are exhausted.
Starving.
Cold.
Some who walk with us
give up,
fall to the ground.
I start to wonder,
Would death be so terrible?
I am willing to find out.
The Czech women not only gave me bread

but they gave me courage.

And hope has returned to partake of the crumbs.

I find strength to try again.

I fall to the ground one more time.

When they kick me

I am still.

Even when the bayonet cuts into my side.

Shhh.

Not a sound.

Not a breath.

Not a motion.

They leave me for dead.

A second time.

HAYSTACK

I crawl

into a haystack.

Sleep.

Hunger wakes me.

As soon as the sun turns off her light,

I sneak into the nearest barn,

steal eggs and potatoes.

Fill my stomach.

During the day

I hide.

Silent.

While farmers work their fields.

I trust no one.

This is how I survive.

The next night it is the same.

More eggs.

More potatoes.

Day three,

an itch makes me careless.

An itch I can't ignore.

I move to scratch my nose.

I make a sound.

I feel my heart beating

loudly

in my chest.

But it is not my heart—

it is footsteps.

They are coming in my direction.

I try to make myself invisible.

An arm reaches in

and grabs me.

I have been found out.

A farmer yanks me from my hiding place.

"See what I've found?" he yells to his mates.

"We will take this Jew to the police."

I am tired of having misfortune for a companion.

A SOLDIER IS COMING

Before I can replay my life,
live and die again,
the silence is broken by explosions.
There is gunfire.
There are trucks.
And there are many voices.
My captor flees.
I am left alone in the field.
A soldier is coming.
I am not ready to die.
I scramble back into the haystack.
The soldier's steps and my heartbeat are in sync.
Shhh.
Not a sound.
Not a breath.
Not a motion.
Fear holds my hand.

SAFE

The soldier speaks.

Not in German. Not in Polish. Not in Czech.

My soldier speaks Yiddish,

the language of my people.

"*Shrek zikh nisht.*

Ikh bin an Amerikaner!"

"Don't be afraid. I am an American."

I fall to the ground in tears.

I do not play dead.

I am alive.

ALIVE.

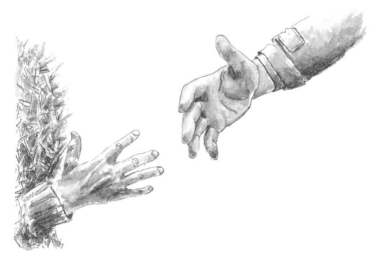

Gloria Moskowitz-Sweet, Hope Anita Smith,
and Michael "Moishe" Moskowitz, 2017

AUTHOR'S NOTE

By Gloria Moskowitz-Sweet

On January 29, 2019, my father died in his home at the age of ninety-two. He needed to tell his story, and like many survivors, struggled to do so for years. Later in life, his stories came, and came, and came. He shared them with his children, his grandchildren, and his friends. He spoke to middle school students, many of whom had never heard about the Holocaust. His is a story of survival, hope, and inspiration. It needs to be told.

My father was born in Kielce, Poland, on August 17, 1926, between the two great wars. Kielce was known for the depth of its hatred of Jews throughout generations. Jews were concentrated in small towns around the city. Despite extreme anti-Semitism, my father always spoke of the safety and love he felt in his home with his mother, Golda; father, Gimple; brother, Saul; and sister, Bella.

In the fall of 1939, when my father was thirteen, Nazi Germany invaded and occupied Poland. By the spring of 1941, about twenty-eight thousand Jews were locked in the Kielce Ghetto. When the ghetto was liquidated in the summer of 1942, his mother and sister were sent to Treblinka, an extermination camp. His father joined an underground Polish resistance and died fighting the Nazis. He and his brother were left to clear the ruins of the ghetto. They were later sent to a forced-labor camp and subsequently separated. My father believed his brother died of typhus in Bergen-Belsen concentration camp at the end of the Holocaust. He never saw any of his family again, but the hope that he would find them sustained him and kept his spirit alive. He endured the forced-labor camps of Skarzysko-Kamienna and Pionki, and the concentration camps of Auschwitz I, Auschwitz

III (also known as Monowitz or Buna), and Buchenwald, as well as two death marches in the winter of 1945.

It was during the first death march, on a cold winter morning in 1945, that my father met the brave women of Czechoslovakia.

As a child, I remember my father asking customers as they came into his dry cleaner's: "Are you from Czechoslovakia?" When I asked why he did this, he would remark that he never met a "Schindler" while he was in the concentration camps, but he will never forget the bravery and kindness of the Czech women who risked their lives. Despite the armed Nazi guards, the women threw loaves of fresh, hot bread to concentration camp prisoners locked inside cattle cars. This story—the image of it raining warm bread—became my fable of hope during my childhood. "Where there is life, there is hope; where there is hope, there is life," my father always said. What he experienced in Czechoslovakia helped restore his belief in the goodness of human beings.

On July 4, 1946, he barely escaped the worst postwar pogrom. He had been staying with about 180 Jewish survivors in a former parish hall in Kielce, Poland. While my father was away searching for family, a mob of Polish residents attacked the parish hall, killing forty-two and injuring up to forty Jewish survivors. My father knew then he had no home in Poland. Later, while in a refugee camp, he asked a stranger leaving for America to post his name in a Jewish newspaper. His uncle Jacob Moskowitz, his father's youngest brother, who had escaped to America before the war, was living in Los Angeles. Uncle Jacob saw my father's name among the survivors and sponsored him to come to America. The only time my father cried when telling his story was when he described seeing his uncle for the first time at the train station, looking back at him with his father's eyes.

Michael "Moishe" Moskowitz and
Leticia Reyes Moskowitz, 1953

My father's second life began in Los Angeles, California. He met my mother, Leticia Reyes, a beautiful Salvadorian woman, in ESL class. Despite speaking different languages and having different religions, they fell in love, married in 1950, and raised four children.

Tragedy and trauma visited my father once again in 1991. His youngest children, Richie, thirty-two, and Brenda, thirty, died six weeks apart. Once again, my father recovered. He lovingly cared for my mother during her long decline with dementia. He fought back bravely from several medical setbacks, including his last heart attack at the age of ninety-one.

My father retired from Baronet Cleaners at the age of ninety-one, where he worked side by side with his son Gary.

Gary Moskowitz, Michael "Moishe" Moskowitz, and Gloria Moskowitz-Sweet, 2017

He found new joy in retirement, the "miracle" of FaceTiming his grandchildren, and in sharing his life story with young people. He inspired all who knew him with the sparkle in his eye, his empathy, his indomitable spirit, and most of all his enduring hope.

Michael "Moishe" Moskowitz with his grandsons (from left: Gabriel, Brandon, and Jesse Sweet; Ian and Luc Moskowitz), 2011